SHONA THE VET
A COAST TO COAST
ADVENTURE

Written & Illustrated by

Catherine Stables

Catherine has been working as a vet for over twenty years, mainly in the beautiful Northeast of Scotland. She started writing stories to amuse her two boys when they were little, the antics of her patients often sneaking into her stories. As well as writing, her other hobbies include basket weaving, drawing wildlife and pet portraits, playing her bagpipes and showing their beloved Shetland sheep at local agricultural shows. She hasn't got a little red helicopter but thinks it would make life a lot easier!

Shona had a special job,
She was a wildlife vet.
Treating Scotland's animals,
And the occasional poorly pet.

Shona travelled coast to coast,
To patients wide and far,
She went by helicopter -
It would take too long by car!

She always took her little dog,
He really loved to fly,
Jock was brown and scruffy,
With a white patch round one eye.

Not long after breakfast
Came the first call of the day.
"There's a salmon trapped
behind a dam!
Let's get on our way."

Landing down at Laggan,
Shona fetched her longest net,
Speaking softly to the salmon,
She said, "There now, don't you fret."

As Shona gently caught her
She felt the fish's body quiver,
She checked the salmon
thoroughly,
Then took her to the river..

"Salmon spawn where they
were born,
Returning every year."
Slowly Shona let her go,
"She'll find her way from here."

"Right, Jock, to the helicopter,
Let's get on our way,
Our next stop is the Moray
Coast,
To a dolphin at Spey Bay."

Shona landed on the shore,
"I think I'll have to swim."
She climbed into her wet suit,
Then slowly waded in.

"Stay here on the shore Jock,
I shoudn't be too long.
Hang on to this life ring, just
In case something goes wrong!"

"I'll have to make some noises,
To draw them over here!"

She 'clicked,' and 'squeaked,'
And 'clicked,' and 'squeaked,'

Until the pod swam near.

One dolphin had a plastic bag,
Wrapped right around her fin!

"Oh how I wish that folk would
Put their rubbish in the bin!"

"One more snip. I've done it Jock!
I've cut the plastic free!"

They stood and watched the dolphins
As they swam back out to sea.

"Off we go again wee Jock,
Across the sea to Skye,
My good friend Anne has found a bird,
Who's struggling to fly."

Flying past the Cuillin Hills,
They landed at Portree,
Anne was there to meet them,
With a welcome flask of tea.

"Oh my word! A puffin!
What a bonny little thing!"

"I found it on the beach,"
said Anne,

"It has a broken wing."

Shona strapped the wing up tight,
"I think that ought to do.
Take the bandage off in three weeks time,
It should be good as new."

"Bye, Anne!" shouted Shona,
As they headed off once more.
"He's in good hands with Anne, Jock,
She'll release him on the shore."

"Last call, Jock, it's to a deer
In the Cairngorm National Park.
We're going to have to hurry though,
Before it gets too dark!"

Shona landed gently,
On a slippy, snowy slope.
"He's just down there," she said
to Jock,

"I'll have to use the rope!"

A deer had stuck his antlers
In the branches of a tree.
"Just hold still now," Shona said,
I'm going to set you free."

She carefully cut the branches off,
And checked he was all right,
He gave his mighty head a shake,
Then bounded out of sight.

"Sometimes stags will drape
their horns
With moss, or bits of twig,
So when they meet their rivals,
They will look all fierce and
big."

"Maybe that's what happened here,
And how this deer got stuck,
I hope next time he dresses up,
He has a bit more luck!"

"Right, Jock, that's us for the day,
   It's time we headed home,
      I'd like a cup of cocoa,
   And you deserve a bone!"

Taking out her journal,
Safely home in Aberdeen,
Shona wrote about the places,
And the animals they had seen.

She took her map of Scotland down
And traced their route with string.
"What a busy day, wee Jock.
What will tomorrow bring?"

ISBN: 978-1-8380379-5-6

Published by Foggie Toddle Books
18 North Main Street, Wigtown DG8 9HL
01988 402896
hello@foggietoddlebooks.co.uk